FIX-IT DUCK

*D*uck drove into my life one morning, smashed into a rock and ever since I haven't been able to get rid of him. Not that I'd really want to.

What I've come to love about Duck is that he's so passionate. There's always something he wants to be doing…until the next thing comes along.

Since moving into his new house, he's been pestering me with his passion for fixing things. The trouble is, when Duck starts fixing things, the problems are only just beginning…

For Clare

First published in hardback in Great Britain by HarperCollins Publishers Ltd in 2001
First published by Collins Picture Books in 2002

3 5 7 9 10 8 6 4
ISBN: 0 00 710624 6

Collins Picture Books is an imprint of the Children's Division, part of HarperCollins Publishers Ltd.
Text and illustrations copyright © Jez Alborough 2001
The author/illustrator asserts the moral right to be identified as the author/illustrator of the work.
A CIP catalogue record for this title is available from the British Library.
The HarperCollins website address is: www.**fire**and**water**.com
Printed in China

Jez Alborough

FIX-IT DUCK

An imprint of HarperCollinsPublishers

Plop! goes the drip that drops in the cup.
Duck looks down and Duck looks up.

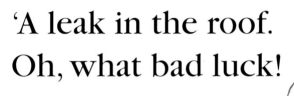

'A leak in the roof.
Oh, what bad luck!

This is a job for…

FIX-IT DUCK.'

He says, 'It's easy to repair.'
But how's he going to reach up there?

He can't climb up –
it's much too steep.

So he drives round to borrow

a ladder from Sheep.

Over the puddles
he hops and he skips

to Sheep's little house,
then, OOPS, he trips!

'Sheep!' calls Duck.
'It's only me.'

And he explains how the rain had dripped in his tea.

When he reaches the part about fixing the leak,
they hear a rattle, creak and a squeak.

'It's my window,' says Sheep,
'it won't close, it's stuck.'

'This is a job for
FIX-IT DUCK.'

He does what he can to close up the gap.
He glues it, screws it and gives it a tap.

'The problem,' says Duck, 'is your glass is too thin.'
'My house,' wails Sheep. 'The rain's coming in!'

'What we need,' says Duck, with a glint in his eye,
'is to pull your house to somewhere dry.

Goat's got a shed. It can shelter inside.
Let's hook up your jeep and go for a ride.

Drive back slowly,
'til I say stop.'

Then all of a sudden,
something goes POP!

'A puncture,' says Duck. 'More bad luck.
We'll have to use my pick-up truck.'

But Sheep's little house won't join to the truck.

'This is a job for…   FIX-IT DUCK.'

'We're off,' says Duck as they speed down the track.

'Slow down on the bends,' calls Sheep from the back.

'Turn left,' he bleats as they skid round a curve.
'Hold tight,' comes the quack as the truck starts to swerve.

And the house should follow behind but instead…

…it unhooks from the truck

and rolls on straight ahead.

When Duck gets to Goat's he starts to explain
why they'd brought Sheep's house which was letting in rain.

'But where is it?' asks Goat.
Then as Duck turns to see,

Frog runs up shouting,
'It's following me!'

'Look up on the hill,'
gasps Goat in dismay.

'It's Sheep,' quacks Duck,
'and he's coming this way!'

'*Run!*' cries Frog.
'He's going to crash!'

'H - E - L - P !' bleats Sheep.

'It's broken,' says Duck. 'What a lot of bad luck.'

'Oh no!' moans Sheep 'not...

FIX-IT

If only he hadn't come calling on me.
If only that rain hadn't dripped in his tea.'

DUCK!

'Not rain,' says Frog, with a shy little cough.

'He forgot to turn his bath tap off.'

Have you heard what happened when Duck was driving home one day?

This is the tale of a duck in a truck –
a truck that was stuck in some yucky brown muck.
A sheep in a jeep and a frog in a bush
saw the truck stuck and gave it a push.
But the truck stayed stuck!
What now, can you guess?
Could a goat in a boat
get them out of this mess?

'Duck in the Truck is packed with all the rhyme, colour,
imagination and humour a young reader could ask for.'
Young Book Trust

'With a nod to Dr Seuss and a wink to John Burningham,
Jez Alborough deals an irresistible lesson in rhyme and
analogy, as well as storytelling, which is hugely entertaining.'
Child Education

'Alborough's pictures are addictive... Duck in the Truck is a
picture book where rhyme, illustration, wit and inventiveness
combine to produce outstanding quality.'
TES Primary

Duck in the Truck

Hardback   0-00-198346-6   £10.99

Paperback   0-00-664717-0   £4.99

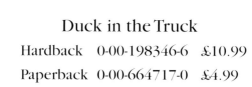

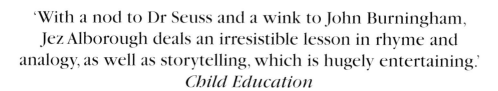